Aa-Choo!

Story by Wendy Orr
Art by Ruth Ohi

**Annick Press
Toronto**

© 1992 Wendy Orr (Text)
© 1992 Ruth Ohi (Art)

Second Printing, January 1992

Annick Press Ltd.
Annick Press gratefully acknowledges the support
of The Canada Council and the Ontario Arts
Council.
Canadian Cataloguing in Publication Data

Orr, Wendy
  Aa-choo!

ISBN 1-55037-209-2 (bound) ISBN 1-55037-208-4 (pbk.)

I. Ohi, Ruth. II. Title.

PS8579.R7A63 1992   jC813′.54   C91-094805-4
PZ7.O77Ac 1992
Distributed in Canada and the USA by:
Firefly Books Ltd.,
250 Sparks Avenue
North York, Ontario
M2H 2S4
The art in this book was rendered in water-
colour. The text has been set in Tiffany light
by Attic Typesetting
Printed and bound in Canda
on acid-free paper by D.W. Friesen & Sons

To James and Susan,
who know how Megan feels

Megan did not want
to get up.

Megan felt hot
   and tired
   and her throat hurt
   and

"AA-CHOO!" said Megan.

"Oh, dear," said Megan's mother.
"You can't go to daycare."

"You can stay home with me," said Megan.
She would stay in bed
and her mother would read her stories
and give her a cuddle
and help dress her dolls.

"I have to go to work," said Megan's mother.
"I have an important meeting today.
I can't stay home with you."

"Daddy can look after me," said Megan.
She would stay in bed
and her father would sing funny songs
and tell silly stories
and cut out paper dolls.

"I have to drive my truck," said Megan's father.
"I have an important load to take today.
I can't stay home with you."

"Mrs. Jackson could stay with me," said Megan.
She would stay in bed
and Mrs. Jackson would come from next door
and bring flowers and pictures of grandchildren
and do magic tricks with cards.

"I have to go bowling," said Mrs. Jackson.
"It's a very important game today.
I can't stay home with Megan."

"You'll have to come to work with me," said her mother.

So Megan packed
    a pillow and a blanket
    a bear and a book
    and a bag of blocks
and went to work with her mother.

Her mother's office was in a big building
    with lots of doors
    and lots of rooms
    and lots of people.

Megan's mother made her a little bed under the desk.
She tucked her in with the teddy
    and read her a story
and stood up quickly when a tall lady came in.
    "It's time for the meeting," said the tall lady.

Megan's mother gave Megan some juice
    and crayons and paper
    and a quick cuddle.
"Be good," said Megan's mother
    and shut the door.

Megan gave her teddy some juice.
She looked at her book.
She built a house with her blocks.
She drew three pictures.
And she felt very bored.

Megan got out of her little bed.
She built a play-house
    with her yellow blanket over the desk
and her mother's chair turned upside down.

She moved the other chairs
    and built a big block town
    with a high wall
in the middle of the room.

The phone rang.
Megan made Teddy say, "Hello,"
but the man said he'd call back later.

She drank a big glass of juice.
Too much juice.
She walked up and down the hall
and peeped in all the doors.

She went into a room
with computers in rows
and a lady typing at each one.

"Are you lost?" said the ladies.
"No," said Megan.
"Do you want your Mommy?"
"No," said Megan.
"Do you want a drink?"
"NO!" said Megan.

"I think I know," said a lady,
and after she had taken Megan to the bathroom
they went back to her mother's office
and played monsters in the play house.

Megan's mother and the people from the meeting
looked surprised when they came back to the office.
Megan's friend stopped being a monster
and went back to her filing.

The next morning Megan felt better.
"Can I go to work with you again?"
she asked —

but Megan's mother did not want
to get up.

Megan's mother felt hot
    and tired
    and her throat hurt
and,

"AA-CHOO!" said Megan's mother.

"Oh, dear," said Megan.
"You can't go to work."

So Megan got a bear and a book:
    "Read Mommy a story," she said to Teddy.

She got an extra blanket and pillow
    and tucked Mommy in.

She made a bowl of cornflakes
    and a glass of juice:

"You can stay home with me," said Megan.